WE HAVEN'T GOT ALL NIGHT, LASS, SO KEEP IT SHORT!

For John, a friend indeed.
(Reverend John Waddington-Feather, 1933–2017.)

WE HAVEN'T GOT ALL NIGHT, LASS, SO KEEP IT SHORT!

Grit

Originally submitted in 2009.
We all wear masks. The question is for how much of the time?! It's good to reveal the 'true you' sometimes and to some person (people).

ARTHUR H. STOCKWELL LTD
Established 1898
www.ahstockwell.co.uk

© Grit, 2022
First published in Great Britain, 2022

The moral rights of the author have been asserted.

All rights reserved.
No part of this publication may be reproduced
or transmitted in any form or by any means,
electronic or mechanical, including photocopy,
recording, or any information storage and
retrieval system, without permission
in writing from the copyright holder.

British Library Cataloguing-in-Publication Data.
A catalogue record for this book is available
from the British Library.

By the same author:
Natural Woman
Maybe Another Time When I'm Not Watching TV!
No One Invited Me & So I Threw My Own!

ISBN 978-0-7223-5137-6
Printed in Great Britain by
Arthur H. Stockwell Ltd
Torrs Park   Ilfracombe
Devon

CONTENTS

Obsessed (Short Story)	9
All Too Powerful	10
20082008	11
A Mixed-up World	12
A Right Collection	13
Lack of Commitment	14
On the Run	15
Two-Way Stream	16
Somewhere Behind the Clouds	17
What It Must Feel Like to Be Full of (Cold) AIDS	18
You're Mental (Short Story)	20
Horseplay (A and B)	21
The Man Who Had Them Burning Cloth from Leeds and Manchester	22
Text It	23
From One Clone to Another	24
One Big Step for Man	25
You've Got to Make It!	26
What Will Be, Will Be	27
Up to Whatever in It	28
Pens	29
What a Lovely Woman (Short Story)	31
Dinner for (One) Three (Short Story)	32
It's Best to Just Duck!	33
When Push Comes to Shove!	34
Yeah – Right, Alice	35
Suffragette City	36
A Reason to Believe (Parts I–III)	37
Made from Love, Conceived in Liberty, Born into a Jungle	38
Beautiful, No Matter What *You* Said	39
Sadly Lacking	40
The Game (Short Story)	42

Fly Like an Eagle	44
Not A–Z	45
Hammerhead	46
Egocentricity	48
Ants in Your Pants	49
Not Going Anywhere	50
A Sitcom Worse Than Death	51
Oh, I Don't Know!	52
Not Exactly Music to the Ears	53
Why Didn't He Finish Her Off? (Short Story)	55
Down at the Bottom of the Lake	61
Damn Near (the) Dead	62
'F.B.I.'	63
Dernier de la Classe	64
IRA	65
The Jump from Petty Thief to High-Security Criminal in One 'Foul' Sweep	66
Hickory Dickory Dead	67
Role Change	68
FFT	69
Twenty-four Black (Birds) Haired Boys (Short Story)	71
Jack and Jill	73
She Always Wanted to Have a Baby	74
Not Groomed	75
The First Cut Is the Deepest	76
(Out of) In Africa	77
Snap, Crackle and Pop	78
To Know One's Place!?!	79
Here to Stay	80
The Million-$ Question	81
Back Door (Short Story)	83
We All Have Qualities!	85
Hungry	86
Today's Society	87
Top Gear	88

Time of Day	89
10B (Short Story)	90
Who Would Have Thought It!	91
Did the Band Turn Up Yet?	92
Just in Time	93
My First, My Last, My Everything (Short Story)	95
You Can't Be Too Careful These Days, Love	97
Curtains	98
Moving in Time	99
Out of the Blue	100
Scream Blue Murder	101
Second Fiddle?	102
When 2 Call It a Day	103
I Don't Need a Second Opinion	104
Have Dreams, Will Fly (Short Story)	106
The (Crossword) Solvers' Boon	107
The Feast	108
What Happened to Summer?	109
Collectively	110
Hello, Mr (Ex) President	111
Tomorrow	111
What a Break (Big Break)!	112
(Men) Woman At Work	113
Short Back and Sides (Short Story)	115
You'll End Up As a Bar of Soap! (Short Story)	116
Shut-Eye	117
Frustration Guaranteed	118
Living in a Box	119
Swan Song (Short Story)	120
Let's Jam It	121
Life – Love = A Waste of One	121
Ménage à Trois	122
Four Green Bottles (A Variation)	123
Give Me a Smile, Then! (Jokes)	124

OBSESSED

She shaved her legs. She shaved his head. In fact, she shaved everything in sight. And she'd had a lot of close shaves since she was a young kid. She'd also played with her dad's shaving cream. She'd plastered it everywhere. She now get's plastered on a Saturday night with something else. More often than not it's with the drink most Russians would die for and probably do because of it!

ALL TOO POWERFUL

Powder blue with paintbrush strokes
of white clouds makes the sky a picture
of breathtaking elegance until the sun
comes and spoils it.

20082008

That's a strange number!
It's not her mobile-phone number.
It's not his serial number.
It's not their car registration number.
It's not your bank-account number.
It's not my lotto numbers.
It's not her student number.
It's not his social-security number.
And it's not the same figure twice.
No, it's today's date.

PS: But, it is the same figure twice. . . .

A MIXED-UP WORLD

In a state of mental confusion,
Marion keeps her guinea pig in the bathroom.
David keeps his onions in the WC.
Angela keeps her gloves in the freezer.
Seb keeps his shoes in the microwave.
Judy keeps her hairbrush in the cake tin.
Chris keeps his wallet in the cellar.
Fran keeps her teeth in the toolbox.
Benjamin keeps his glasses in the garden shed.
Grace keeps her keys in the middle drawer
of the bedside cabinet in the guest room painted pink.
Tom keeps his boxer shorts at Lucy's.
Where does Jillian keep her hat?

A RIGHT COLLECTION

Little Miss Wise (. . . full of good advice).
Little Miss Sunshine (. . . brightens up the day).
Little Miss Naughty (. . . loves to seduce).
Little Miss Neat (. . . in just about everything).
Little Miss Trouble (. . . as perceived by others).
Little Miss Helpful (. . . with as many and as often as possible).
Little Miss Quick (. . . off the mark).
Little Miss Busy (. . . always running).
Little Miss Tidy (. . . in every room).
Little Miss Shy (. . . until the ice breaks).
Little Miss Fun (. . . loving).
Little Miss Chatterbox (. . . who always has a lot that needs
            saying).
Little Miss Lucky (. . . to be in this world here and now).

LACK OF COMMITMENT

I don't want your phone that never rings.
I don't want your letter that never finds my box.
I don't want your present that never gets wrapped.
I don't want your alibi that never holds up.
I want your love!

ON THE RUN

Who is?
The fugitive?
The band?
The refugee?
The perpetrator?
The man who can't pay his debts?
The water?
No, my nose,
Cos I'm up to my ears in this cold!

TWO-WAY STREAM

The motivating force behind *getting* the appropriate help is to be able to *give* the appropriate help in return.

SOMEWHERE BEHIND THE CLOUDS

You open your eyes.
Are you here?
Everyone is watching.

Look into my eyes.
Feel the love.
Hopelessly lost in your chemistry.
It's easy to see.

Dead flowers floating on top of hot water.
Was it?
Let me go now.
Don't control me.

I'm left here in the dark.
But no one cares.
Cos I'm an idiot.

WHAT IT MUST FEEL LIKE TO BE FULL OF (COLD) AIDS

Oh my God, why me?
I only made one mistake in my life
and it's going to cost me it.
What will my *mum* think when she knows? he said.

No, no – quick, I must end it.
I don't know how to – never done this
kind of thing before.
I want to cry a thousand tears
but the well's dry – why?
Help me . . . someone!

Better keep it to myself,
otherwise society will hate me.
The monster will take it all away –
my loved ones, my disco friends,
my daily work, my hopes of living my dreams – stop!

My skull is pressing against my pink flesh.
All I see is red – I loved that
colour to death as a kid.
LIFE, life is what I desire,
so I'll put the blade away until the next
attack of PANIC, PANIC, PANIC, PANIC, PANIC,
PANIC, panic, panic, panic, pani . . . c,
pani . . . c, pani . . .
(drained of strength).

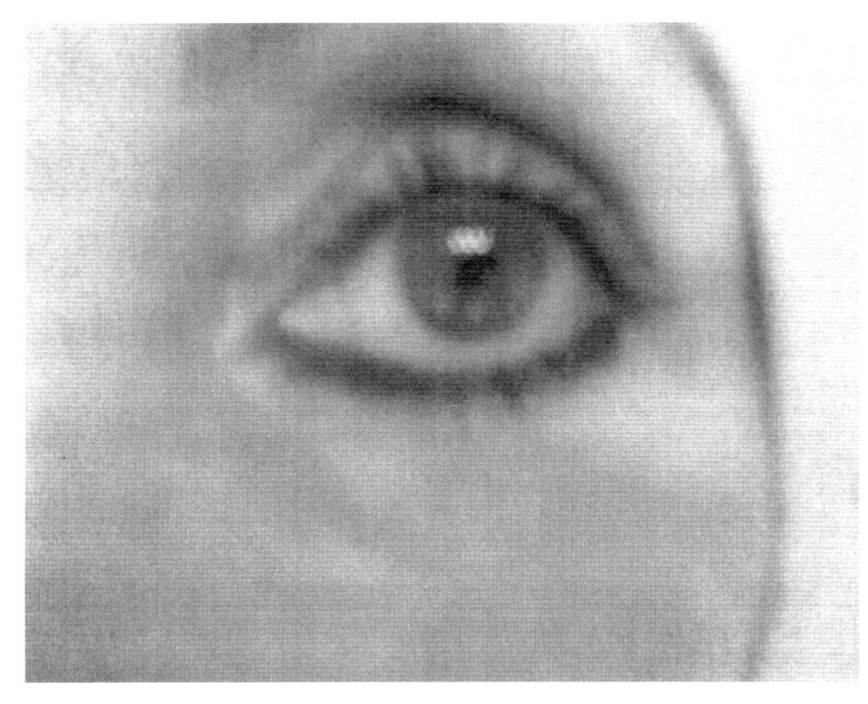

YOU'D BETTER KEEP YOUR EYE ON IT!

YOU'RE MENTAL

She wouldn't go anywhere near the institute. Not even to borrow something. She always said that they would probably keep her there if she did! To put her in her rightful place. That was it. He'd wanted it for years. His greatest wish. The nurse turned to speak to him. He'd gone. He had her where he wanted her. Nothing more to discuss. Of course, he'd never talked about it . . . !

HORSEPLAY (A)

They say you shouldn't look a gift horse in the mouth. So, why have you been looking at my teeth for the past twenty minutes instead of enjoying this magical moment?

HORSEPLAY (B)

I work like a horse,
but get treated like a mule. . . .

THE MAN WHO HAD THEM BURNING CLOTH FROM LEEDS AND MANCHESTER (INDIA)

"Look at him!"
"I can see the British shaking now!"
And how he did shake them,
as well as the salt.
And it wasn't just a pinch that did it.
Married at thirteen.
Bad luck to have to marry that young.
Must have been a Friday.
He wasn't only spinning his wheel,
he was dealing with it.
"Homespun is best."
He sported it around his loins often enough.
A staff in his hand to lead his flock.
"An eye for an eye makes blind," he said.
Well, he did wear glasses . . .
And he was shot between them.
In the end, it was a tooth for a tooth,
don't you think?
There were some who thought his were bad. . . .

TEXT IT

What's one of the hardest things
to get people to do these days?
To talk!
It's *in* to text.
But, what about the man whose fingers
are afflicted with rheumatism?
Or, the woman who shakes from
head to toe with Parkinsonism?
Or, the girl who feels nothing
from the neck downwards?
Are they *out*?!

FROM ONE CLONE TO ANOTHER

It's about being yourself.
Letting your inner self out.
It's what makes you **different** from me,
me from him, him from her, her from them,
them from us, us from everybody else!
"Who wants to be a millionaire?"
was once the question on her lips.
But "Who wants to be a robot?"
is the question on mine.
That's what will make you the **same** as me,
me as him, him as her, her as them,
them as us, us as everybody else!
But, who wants to be a robot?
To leave the capsule if we dare?
Who wants to be a robot?
I don't! I want my own face.
But the heat is on.
The electronic tidal wave is surging upon us.
And it electrifies even society's smallest.
I will always dance, and out of line.

ONE BIG STEP FOR MAN

"Never try, never fail!"
It's a damn good job that those who gave us
the light bulb,
the telephone,
the aeroplane,
the television,
the hairdryer,
the microscope,
the automobile,
the dentist's drill
did it nevertheless!

YOU'VE GOT TO MAKE IT!

To put it bluntly,
        discourteously,
        frankly,
        explicitly,
        brusquely,
        rudely, you had better sharpen up;
                otherwise you'll be a failure,
                              fiasco,
                              nonperformer,
                              washout,
                              no-hoper,
                              dead duck!

WHAT WILL BE, WILL BE

Some will be doctors, teachers, builders, hairdressers, bankers, dancers, gardeners, nurses, prostitutes, shop assistants, architects, models, carpenters, cleaners, lecturers, rock stars, refuse collectors, movie directors, scientists, lawyers, cordon-bleu chefs. . . .

But the happiest of all will be himself (herself)!

UP TO WHATEVER IN IT

Stuck in the inextricable quicksand.
Stuck in a prison cell.
Stuck in a marriage.
Stuck between the boundries (Mum and Dad set).
Stuck in the ice.
Stuck in the mud.
Stuck in a rut.
Stuck in the mind.
Stuck in Parma (well as long as there's the ham . . . !)
We are never quite free
in this life, are we?!

PENS

They're all the same.
Row upon row.
Metal which chills.
Remains of scarecrows
all over the floor.
Continuous light of bulb.
No room to swing a cat.
Prison.
Home to those poor sacred ones.

WHO'S NEXT?

WHAT A LOVELY WOMAN

What a lovely woman. That's what they used to say before she snapped his neck. It happened all so quick. She didn't realise how much strength she had in those two hands of hers. It's amazing just what you can do if you are driven to it. She had been.

DINNER FOR (ONE) THREE

They frightened the life out of her. She'd only been there a couple of minutes before they were sniffing at her legs. They'd quickly surrounded her. Who had opened the door? She'd actually preferred looking at the three of them from the other side of the glass! She was soon escorted into the basement. The strange old lady and her nurse in white made her nervous, and someone kept turning the light off! She wasn't there long. Thrown to the dogs and then out into the night. Still, she'd have to go back again, if only to collect her jacket!

IT'S BEST TO JUST DUCK!

You'd better move since you're in the line of fire.
I've always been in that!
Well, at least for as long as I can remember.
I have had all sorts thrown at me:
handballs, crayons, confetti, apples, footballs, kisses,
snow, tomatoes, rice, compliments, tantrums,
stones, fits and parties.
The book!
Life is tough! And, I do get going . . . !

WHEN PUSH COMES TO SHOVE!

Tackling your own members
is not my idea of being a team,
or in the spirit . . . !

YEAH – RIGHT, ALICE

School's out . . .
But never for me.
So, what do I do
with all this knowledge?
Do I share it?
Do I auction it off?
Do I use it for my shopping lists?
Do I sit on it?
Do I take it to the grave?
Do I put it to good use?
That would make more sense,
now, wouldn't it!!

SUFFRAGETTE CITY

I'm definitely like those ladies.
I fight for mine, as they did back in the(ir) day.
They risked their necks
for their sake and that of others.
They were treated roughly.
They were jeered at.
They chained themselves to things.
What's the difference?
Not much.
I don't budge from the spot either!

A REASON TO BELIEVE

I
If at first you don't succeed, try, try again.
That makes three tries.
Why do I always have to try more?

II
"All good things come to an end,"
said the RC to the Protestant.
And what about the bad things?
Do they?
Cos for your information, I've had more than my fair share!

III
A stitch in time saves nine.
How many does a stitch behind time save?
Probably more (if well planned).

MADE FROM LOVE, CONCEIVED IN LIBERTY, BORN INTO A JUNGLE

You're equal on 'day one.' But then that's it! And then it matters. What colour skin/hair/eyes you have. What your father does. If you stutter. If you're short in stature and sight. If your mother is at home part-time, full time or any time! If you have two feet. If both livers function. What kind of people your grandparents were, and theirs before them. How close to normal your blood pressure is. What tendencies you have, sexual and otherwise. What you want 'to be, or not to be' in the words of Hamlet's creator.

BEAUTIFUL, NO MATTER WHAT *YOU* SAID

"You won't make the catwalk, I'm afraid."
Your skin's as white as cheese.
You've got a squint.
Your hair's thin.
One hip's higher than the other, and,
you don't walk straight.
You've got hammer toes.
You've got far too many freckles.
Your legs are not pipe-cleaner thin.
Your breasts are the size of nuts.

Anything else wrong with me whilst *you* are at it?

SADLY LACKING

"People are beautiful because we love them."
So, does that mean that that group of
slanderous,
low-down,
surly,
back-stabbing,
spiteful
people over there
don't get any?

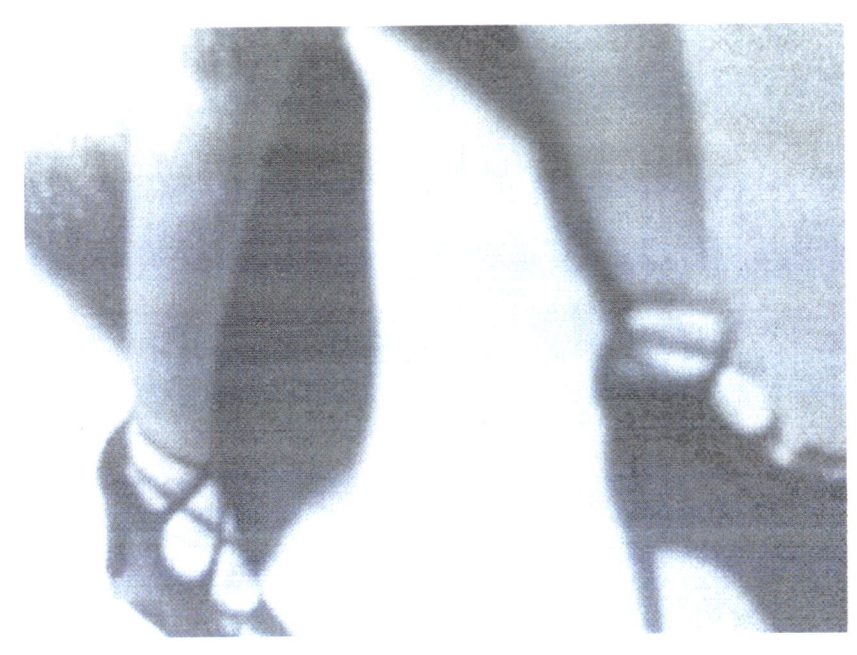

A RIGHT FAUX PAS!

THE GAME

He opened the door. He froze. She was really giving it some on his couch. He just stood and stared. She was amazing. She ran her fingers over her thighs. She ran her fingers over his thighs and then she pushed them in his mouth. Her eyes were totally focused on him. They were all over him. Up and down, like they were.

He eventually did come to his senses. So, he'd merely been a part of it! The game. It was now over. He could have turned. He didn't. He just marched straight forward and whacked both of them.

The playmate managed to run in the end. She didn't. She now had to play his game. He would show no mercy. She reluctantly told him that they'd been at it for three hours before he arrived on the scene.

"Nice," he said.

So he chose to treble it. But not on the couch this time. He chose the back seat of her car. That was where he liked it best. She performed excellently in the car. So off they drove.

It was quiet and secluded. She'd been forced to dress. She thought she'd now have to undress. But he didn't give her the chance. He just ripped it all off. For her it was a strange combination of excitement and fear. He was very turned on. And she was going to be totally turned off. He just kept working her.

"No rest for the wicked," he said aloud.

He got his satisfaction over and over again. And then quite suddenly and as if someone had pushed a button he drove her and the car out from under the tree and straight over the cliff. They flew like eagles. There was no sea though.

It was a violent end to a violent day for all of them.

'Let's start as we mean to carry on' took on a whole new and warped meaning for him.

Even in the face of it she wouldn't say how long she'd been carrying on. That secret went with them.

FLY LIKE AN EAGLE

I did.
But I flew off.
To warmer climbs?
No.
To the land of beer and sausage and sauerkraut!
I floated for ages.
Eventually I reached heights.
And then I plummeted.
A slow process of restoration.
Then offspring.
Another flight cross-border.
To warmer climbs?
No.
To the Land of the Midnight Sun, people born on skis and those who still enjoy the whale
on the platter *instead* of roaming the ocean.

NOT A – Z

"From Paris to Berlin . . ."
In my case, from Poznan.
Two different worlds in one day actually.
The former, cute with a touch of *Dolce Vita*.
The latter, a lively hubbub.
Inappropriately the taxi driver
didn't hear well!
At the hotel reception desk
some forgotten poster dressed in cream.
"They used to know me here"
were the words from the lips of that
irritated older species of a dragoness.
Alas, the room service had already gone for the day.
Rien de va plus!
Happily the churning of my stomach
didn't keep me from my state of slumber. . . .

HAMMERHEAD (1975–1980)

Well, he liked girls.
And he did have a ripping time!
Every time.
When he wasn't contained, that is.
And he left his mark.
Size 7.

He moved around.
Up and down the country.
He often wrote, letters.
We saw them, nationwide.
And then there was a voice.
We heard it on tape.
You could ring in.

Hammer and (tongs) knives.
Wide open.
A right crusade.
Six years divided by thirteen chicks.
A bad track record by all accounts.
Not moral, and he could have dug their graves.

He had mud on his boots.
A great big disgrace.
Because they were oblivious.
They were rubber.
And key.
But a well-appointed house meant that Peter was out of it.

Girls, girls, girls!
Or maybe he didn't like them?!
That was it, a right blow!
But then, by some stroke, luck took him in.
He'd been told to clean the streets,
but not with a brush.

They kept relocating him.
Just to be safe.
But, we were not.
Women of all walks felt horror on the streets after dark.
Didn't notice how near he parked!!!
He probably had a list.
Could have been on it.
But then again, I merely sold the stuff you spin with
and I *had* finished my studies (towards the back end). . . .

EGOCENTRICITY

"There is nothing one man
will not do for another."
And, more to the point,
there is nothing one man
will do for another.
Who knows, he might
just have it better (than him)!

ANTS IN YOUR PANTS

4 × 4 ants.
Four ants were almost breaking their (own) necks
to get to the juicy leaf first.
Four ants were breaking <u>their</u> necks
to get to the juicy leaf first.
Four ants were breaking the necks of the first eight
to get to the juicy leaf first.
Four ants (the very same) were puking all over the place
cos they ate up the whole bloody caboodle.
Well, it just served that lot right.
One for all, but not all for one!
Or should I say four?

NOT GOING ANYWHERE

I'm going nowhere.
Not in any direction.
Not up.
Not down.
Not to the left.
Not to the right.
Not backwards.
Not forwards.
I'm stuck in the (middle) muddle!
It seems no one can help me, not even Steeley.
He's supposed to be in it with me,
but so far I'm going it alone.
A bit like the last of the Mohicans, one might say.
A true fighter. A survivor.
Certainly not majority.
Not even minority.
Just a one (wo)man band who is floundering
from one mistake to another.

Or is she?

A SITCOM WORSE THAN DEATH

I'd rather my kids and I were starving in Biafra
than going through this here!
What's the difference?
Over there you're in a hopeless situation
and you can't help yourself.
Over here you can, but no one will . . .
help me to help myself!

At least they didn't when I wrote this!

OH, I DON'T KNOW!

If in doubt

* read the instructions
* call to ask
* take another route
* don't turn up
* go early
* look the other way
* hide it
* deny it
* laugh (?)

* do it anyway (?!)

NOT EXACTLY MUSIC TO THE EARS

"You know I don't talk much,
except to myself,"
cos no one in this godforsaken life is listening to me, Bryan.

A SIGHT FOR SORE EYES IF EVER THERE WAS ONE!

WHY DIDN'T HE FINISH HER OFF?

"Bloody hell! She's still alive."

"Sid, Sid! Get over here. This one's not dead!"

"All right, Daniel, keep your rag on. I told you not to drink so much at lunch."

"Oh shit! You're right. Get on the blower *now* for an ambulance."

Daniel got straight through to the hospital, but not to the lady on the other end of the phone. What him being new to the job had to do with the fact that he needed someone to come around without delay was beyond him. He was beginning to get somewhat tired of having to prove that just because he had a different accent it didn't mean that he was incompetent! He'd been in the force for fifteen years and had certainly seen his fair share of the stuff nightmares are made of. Anyway, it was a good job he had developed a thick skin.

"I can't for the life of me think why he didn't finish her off! She'll not get over this in a bunch of Sundays, Sid."

"Oh, you'd be amazed, lad. Don't write her off yet. All that water won't have done her much good though, that's for sure. What an ordeal! And what in heaven's name is she doing with that big knife? She hasn't got much on under that coat either! Those shoes need checking out too. Flashy, they are. Can't get that kind of shoes around here."

Sid continued to look for anything in the way of evidence he could get his hands on, but Daniel was ready to drive back to the station. He was walking briskly up the hill from the canal when he saw a man in a rather scruffy-looking raincoat hanging around the church graveyard.
  "Hey, you! Can I have a quick word?"
  The man seemed oblivious to the fact that Daniel was talking to him. Then, all at once, he turned round. Daniel almost choked. He knew that he had seen him before, but could not begin to think where.
  "Can you tell me something about the young woman we found tied up in the lake? Seen or heard anything?"
  "No, I mind my own business, I do! But I suppose you're thinking that it is the same monster who bumped off the three sisters? Am I right? Well, you are wrong. You are completely on the wrong track."
  Daniel was looking somewhat confused.
  "You've got to look closer to home! He's been among you for years, you just didn't know it. It's amazing how a bit of power can go to one's head! How's Penny doing? I miss her. She's a bit of all right, that lass. She's not like the rest of them. She knows how to make a man feel good. Well, lad, you ask Penny why she's missing a toe and has a scar as long as the M1 across her back! You ask Penny why she lisps and can't get a cup of hot tea down her! You'd better ask her . . ."
  Before Daniel could say anything, the man in the raincoat wiped the tear from his eye and rushed off in the direction of the library.
  "This whole thing is getting more bizarre by the

minute," Daniel said to himself as he was searching for his car keys in his trouser pocket. You see, Penny fell out of a third-floor apartment window the previous Monday and had been lying in a coma ever since.

Well, he never did find those car keys. He must have left them somewhere or the man in the raincoat could have taken them. He thought that was just too silly though. It couldn't possibly happen to him, him being a policeman.

"What is this world coming to?" he said to himself as he now frantically tried to find his mobile phone. It didn't take him long to get hold of a colleague named Gavin, who then collected him and drove him to the station in a jiffy. Although Gavin wanted to play out, Daniel had a pile of work to catch up on. He declined. Gavin didn't like it one bit.

"You're getting to be a right bore, you are," he said.

Daniel didn't say much. He didn't want to get into yet another row with Gavin. 'Who wants to go out with a guy who only likes the sound of his own voice and merely has one topic of conversation,' he thought to himself. He'd tried a few interesting positions himself, but Gavin beat him hands down when it came to experimenting with things and women.

"Have one for me" was his reply eventually.

Gavin grabbed his rather worn-out leather gloves and stormed off in a huff.

It was pretty dark in the office and there was this almost deadly hush. It seemed like everyone had gone for the day, only to be called back in again, as was usually the case. He didn't mind being on call. Part of his duty, it was. His girlfriends didn't quite see it that way. They never lasted long. Apart from Penny. He too was under her spell. But, right now she was under one herself in that hospital bed across the other side of town.

"Trick or treat, mate?" a voice bellowed from behind him.

He almost broke his teeth on the pencil he had been gnawing at whilst concentrating on what had been one of his most challenging cases to date. He had never been interested much in Halloween. He didn't even know that it was Halloween. Well, he did now.

"Christ, you nearly scared the life out of me, Tom!"

Tom laughed his head off. There was more than a hint of sarcasm in his voice. He looked very sinister in that mask. For Daniel it was the voice that gave him away.

"What the heck is wrong with you, mate? The job getting to you, is it?"

Daniel could hear his old boss in Chester saying: "It's part and parcel of it, lad."

"You've got no bottle, that's what it is" was the last thing Tom said before he disappeared round the corner. The one he must have come from.

Daniel had just about stopped sweating like a pig when Tom walked past, saying, "Hi. What are you up to at this late hour?"

Daniel was dumbfounded and at the same time irritated. So, who was the man in the mask?

Once he was out of the main door his thoughts flew to Penny. He couldn't keep himself from her bedside and he didn't. She was so beautiful. He didn't know whether to laugh or cry. He didn't do either. He just stared at her in awe. He'd never felt this way before. He didn't want anyone else near her – not the man in the raincoat, not his boss. . . . He always found an excuse to touch her!

After putting her favourite flowers to rest on the table in front of the window he sat and ran his fingers over her slim ones. The feel of her skin made him go weak again. She twitched. She opened her eyes, albeit for a short, and the last, time. The piercing sound of the machine monitoring her heart was still fresh in his ears for weeks after.

He couldn't bear it. He took three days off. He didn't do much but stare at one empty beer bottle after the other. His trying to drown his sorrows was an understatement. All he could think of was kissing her neck, running his hands over her black lace stocking tops and touching the spot which made her so happy. He'd done it as often as he could. She never said no.

He'd used his year's supply of tissues in one afternoon. Not the first afternoon, but the second. It had taken a while to sink in. The only woman he'd ever adored had just slipped from him, and the world. He didn't care about the world. But the world cared about him – at least a little part of it. It wasn't long before a call came in on his mobile from the station telling him how sorry they all were, how they understood his need for some space, but that he'd have to get his bottom back into the office quick. He spruced himself up as best he could and drove in swiftly, as if in a trance. He hadn't been there for more than forty-five minutes when he felt that he just had to get some fresh air or suffocate! He decided to buy a *caffè latte* from his usual haunt. The minute he stepped over the threshold he knew it was him.

The man in the raincoat turned to the side immediately when Daniel entered the shop. Daniel tried to avoid him, but had no choice but to look at him.

"Heard from Penny?" he shouted across.

"She never actually confided in you, did she? I don't suppose you did much talking! Quite an animal, I believe!"

Daniel went just about every shade of red under the sun. It was obvious that this man knew a lot more than first met the eye. Daniel was beginning to feel uncomfortable in his presence.

"Well, I'm happy to say that I got a *very* interesting letter from her only yesterday."

At that point the man looked Daniel straight in the eye and said, "That's what you get for not believing her! It will haunt you. Mark my words, it will haunt you."

DOWN AT THE BOTTOM OF THE LAKE

Down at the bottom of the lake there were
sixteen dead bodies festering in the mud.
One was missing a leg.
One had a ring on the second finger of the right hand.
One had sharp toenails.
One had a knife in the back.
One had a red skirt on.
One had bulging biceps.
One had an ear ripped off.
One had green eyes.
One had a scar from the left hip to the left knee.
One had diamond earrings.
One had barbed wire around the hands and feet.
One had bad teeth.
One had a look of horror.
One had a cut throat.
One had a black eye.
One wasn't quite dead!

DAMN NEAR (THE) DEAD

I'm in here – the land of the living.
Over there it's the resting place of the weary souls.
Those who went too soon.
Those in pain.
Those who lost count of the days.
Those who had no choice – or chance, for that matter.
Those who served.
Those who took it.
Those who had lost it.
Those who had no one.
Those who were loved.
Those no one knew.
Those splashed all over.
Those who were criticised.
Those who pined.
Those who climbed the ladder.
Those who came from afar.
Those who were silenced.

Too close for comfort?

'F.B.I.'

It's plastered across your chest.
You stand on the stairs of success?
You watch the moves of many to hip hop and techno.
For what?
Are you casting, investigation or just **F**lipping **B**ad **I**nside?

DERNIER DE LA CLASSE

But they're always the top actually.
They're the ones who

* talk far too much and miss more
cos they've just got such an imagination,

* live alone with Mum, who is fighting with
social services every week to put
margarine on the . . . ?

*spray their ideas all over town
cos they can't afford the paper to graffiti them on to,

* have had Dad or some uncle or other on them far
more times than they'd care to remember
or whisper to anyone (else . . .),

* cringe at the very sight/thought of dog dirt
cos they've had excretion thrust down
their backs too often *après* (ski) school,

* have a cracking time and then withdraw
and withdraw and withdraw (into a corner or something),

* have seen too many bottoms of too many
beer bottles before going pub(l)ic,

* have 'no crib for a bed' every (school) night of the week.

Aces when it comes to knowing the score!

IRA (NORTHERN IRELAND – 1970s)

Inexcusable **R**uthless **A**ctions.

Penny for her thoughts, *then*.

She was in the prime of her
young life back in
three score years and eleven.

She wasn't 'leaning on the
lamppost at the corner of the street';
she was tied, tarred and feathered to it!

In the limelight she was, that sticky
'feathered chorister'.

Her larynx was not the only
thing inflamed.

Dressed to kill.

Unbelievably lucky not to have been!

Post-positive wave of terror,
not only in the road which fell.

Penny for her thoughts, *now*.

Penny for theirs, those inflictors
of such **I**rately **R**epulsive **A**mmunition.

Not much compensation, is it,
a penny?!!

THE JUMP FROM PETTY THIEF TO HIGH-SECURITY CRIMINAL IN ONE 'FOUL' SWEEP (NORTHERN IRELAND – 1974)

"I'll be back when I'm a millionaire, Gran."
Well, he got that one wrong didn't he!
The mighty sum of £200,000.00
A far cry from a million.
And, what did he do to get it?
Gave away fifteen years of his precious time,
for something he hadn't dreamt of doing …..

for a trillion!

HICKORY DICKORY DEAD
(NORTHERN IRELAND – 2009)

The clock struck after twelve (× 12).
The mouse came out of the woodwork.
Once more 'the stuttering rifles' rapid rattle'.
There was no running.
Just quick squirts.
Much was shed.
Blood and tears, no sweat.
Trouble was about.
The others fled.
To the streets.
There were banners.
There were colleagues.
And there was a silence.
That was also deadly.
They had shut up shop (and other establishments).
End of day.
End of an era, despicably.
Is it going to strike again?
Will it be one (day, week, month, year, decade or century) before it crawls back in?
Will they cry out?
There's a need for resuscitation.
Some successful mouth-to-mouth.
Kick it in!
No need for more street-fighting years.
Or appalling carnage.
We'll play no such 'Anthem for doomed youth'.
Don't want them to pay.
Want to hear them sing.

ROLE CHANGE

Pigs might fly.
Dogs might laugh (to see sport).
Snakes might cook.
Cats might play fiddles.
Rabbits might dance.
Cows might jump (over the moon).
Snails might skate.
Dishes might run away (with spoons).
People might grow up.
One can always live in hope!

FFT

Food for thought.

I *thought for* one minute that
you didn't like my *food.*

I *thought* you said you'd go
out *for* some *food?*

I couldn't think of *food*
for the *thought* of you!

How does the *thought* of
flying to London *for* a
plateful of your favourite
food strike you?

He scoffed that *food* down
like he had no other *thought*
but *for* grub.

The *food* poisoning was *thought*
to have been detected by
the health inspector *for*
more than two months before
he took any action.

Food and drink *for* those who *thought.*

WELL, I'M LOOKING THROUGH THEM, BUT THEY'RE NOT TINTED AND WHAT I'M LOOKING AT ISN'T ROSY!

TWENTY-FOUR BLACK (BIRDS) HAIRED BOYS

She just loved boys with blond hair. And he knew it. He didn't have blond hair. And he was going to make sure that no one with blond hair would have her between his sheets. Most certainly not for more than a night. He thought that he could block it. Best-case scenario: they wouldn't even want one night, he thought. That's all it took actually. One night. And then they were hooked, for all time's sake.

He was fit for nothing after she'd finished with him. At least that was what he was telling everyone. It was the usual cry-baby stuff. He was the world's best at that. And he'd try anything to still be able to control her. He was a control freak if ever there was one. Even though he should have buried the hatchet long since, he was still dreaming up ways to make her believe that he had control over her phones and her PC. And everywhere she went she felt that his eyes were upon her. And there were comments. Many comments.

She loved art. Going to art galleries for hours on end was one of her hobbies. In fact, it was quite a passion. She was pleasantly surprised to receive an invitation to the opening of a new exhibition at her favourite one over on the other side of town. She didn't speak to colleagues at work about it. She kept her private life just that – *very* private.

When the day arrived she changed into some trendy gear and headed off. It didn't take her long to get there. She walked up the steps and in through the heavy brown doors. The lady keeping an eye on the coats and jackets gave her a nice smile. The man standing at the bottom of the stairs leading up to the exhibition didn't. She was still puzzled when she turned the corner at the top of the third flight of marble. But it soon turned to shock. The little room across was filled with row upon row of shop-window dummies. They were dressed in white cloaks only, had black hair and had masks with his boyish face on them. All twenty-four of them were staring right at her and sniggering, as he used to. The room was so crowded. The air was thin, being directly under the roof. She was dizzy. She was gasping for air. She fell backwards and hit her head on the small glass table.

It was a shame no one came. She lay there for hours. He'd arranged for a private showing. And, he did. He showed her. He was still in control. It was a small gathering at the funeral. Only him and her. And then there was only him. She disappeared into the flames in her white cloak, black wig and mask.

"She certainly didn't have anything to snigger about" was the comment the funeral director made.

He kept thinking about it as he sat in his counting house later in the day. Counting the money she'd saved 'for a rainy day' in a joint savings account. She hadn't been able to find the book. But, he had. And it was raining for the umpteenth time that month.

JACK AND JILL

This is the house that Jack built.
This is the meal that Jill threw together.
This is the window that Jack broke.
This is the jacket that Jill ripped.
This is the vase that Jack smashed.
This is the book that Jill burned.
This is the drink that Jack laced.
This is the TV set that Jill pushed over.
This is the telephone wire that Jack cut.
This is the wall that Jill scratched at.

Jack and Jill don't get on, do they?!

PS: What do you think they needed the pail and water for?

SHE ALWAYS WANTED TO HAVE A BABY

Once upon a time
I had a perfect figure.
You were born
and now I don't!

Once upon a time
I had a dream job.
You were born
and now I haven't!

Once upon a time
I could get my 'fun' just when I wanted it.
You were born
and now I can't!

Hey, missus, are you having a bad hair day or something?!

NOT GROOMED

She doesn't wash her hair often enough!
Well, if I had done you wouldn't be sat reading this. . . .

THE FIRST CUT IS THE DEEPEST

They threw her out
like she was nothing.
That little lamb,
unable to once more
find her feet.
Pain-stricken.
For hours, for days,
for weeks, for months,
for years, forever!
"The first cut is the deepest,
baby, I know" –
But you did it anyway,
aided and abetted by
unsparing females.

(OUT OF) IN AFRICA

Lambs who turn into sheep
are no longer meek nor mild.
Some flee to spare.
Far and few between.
Operation mutilation.
A far cry from human rights,
women's rights or anything else that's right!
Not cries, but screams,
which shiver to the bone.
Incomprehensible to me
how those great men
appear to keep their eyes so tightly
closed to this treasure trail.
Little gems hauled to an
off-the-beaten-track reception of old knives.
The stash?
A store of nightmares, shame, enmity and numbness.
"If only it had been numb," they say.
"If only it were still!" they sob.

SNAP, CRACKLE AND POP

Min(e)d where you walk.
Mind where . . .
Bang!
Clouds of dust.
Dirt springing up all over the place,
and in her face.
An arm.
His arm!
She heard the bone snap.
She smelt the flesh and blood crackle.
She saw the blisters pop and weep,
as she too wept.
Kids like to try new things, don't they!
Too bad there are so many
old souvenirs still lying
around such plots of land.

Don't give her that cereal any more.
For the death of him, she can't seem to get it down.

TO KNOW ONE'S PLACE!?!

I'm here (in the *Book*),
Where are you (*Mark*)?

HERE TO STAY

"You're going nowhere," she said.
"You're not packing that case."
"You're not taking that plane."
"You're not moving in with her."
"You're not parking her car."
"You're not cancelling my card."
"You're not giving her everything her heart desires."
"You're not massaging her feet."
"You're not speaking sweetly into her phone."
"You're not mixing her favourite cocktail."
"You're not reserving a table for her (and you)
in the trendiest restaurant in town."
"You're not zipping up her dress."
"You're not stroking her hair."
"You're not kissing her sensous lips."
"You're not holding her in your arms for hours on end."
"You're not making her beg for more."
"You're not waking her with a smile."

"Just try . . . !"

THE MILLION-$ QUESTION

"Why be you when you can be new?"
Why be mad when you can be glad?
Why be rude when you can change your mood?
Why be a snake when you can give and take?
Why be a real swine when you can be fine?
We all like a change, and to see one!

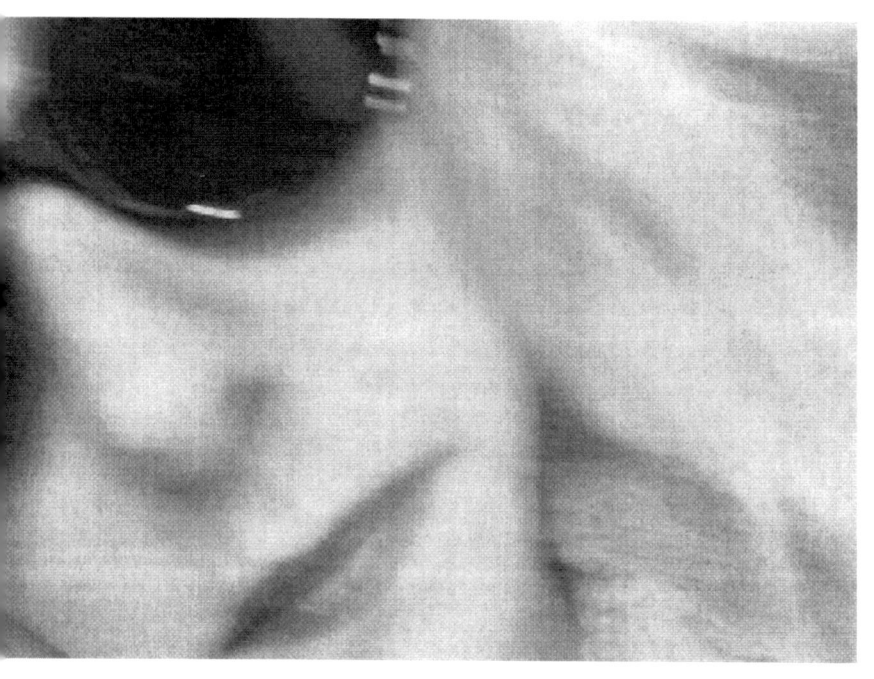

GO ON, TRY AND KEEP ME IN THE DARK, BUT I'LL FIND THE SWITCH AT SOME POINT!

BACK DOOR

"Hi. It's Paul."

"Meet me at the warehouse at eleven."

"Back door, as usual."

"Can't wait to get you into bed."

Dawn hadn't seen Paul for ages. He'd been away on one of his 'around the globe in ten days' trips again and, otherwise, he'd been running from one exhibition to the next in an attempt to work himself into the ground. It had been a long day at the office and she was feeling pretty done in, but getting Paul's message was like a breath of fresh air. She adored him. And that feeling was mutual.

She slipped into the bath, almost ignoring just how hot the water was. She instinctively forgot to add the cold. Her mind was a million miles away. It was racing from one rendezvous to another.

She wasn't in the water for long. She'd decided to wear his favourite outfit. It was a little tight, but he liked that. Throwing it on was her next move. She was quick at dressing. Of course he preferred her not to cover it all up.

In her rush to leave the apartment she hadn't seen the canister strategically placed on the second-from-the-top step. She fell down the whole flight. The blow to her head on the way down hurt her and the one at the bottom instantly killed her. She was lying in a sea of blood in no time. Her limbs were a tangled heap.

It was not too long before the police arrived. Paul had been so impatient to see her that he had driven round to collect her. He wanted to surprise her. He was the one who got the surprise. The surprise of his life, one might say.

He just managed to contact the Yard after going into a state of shock. The hallway was a right mess as well as being full to the brim with coppers soon after. They all said how serene she looked! As pretty as a picture. And they did take a lot. They certainly wanted her on record.

His art friends were extremely comforting.

"It's good to have friends at a time like this," he said to his best one.

But it isn't the case when they caused it! They didn't like her from the start. He saw far too much of her, they thought. But he didn't. He saw too much of *them*. They had a strong hold.

He never knew. He wouldn't know until they found the culprit. That was years later. They camouflaged it so very well. In the meantime he'd moved in with the main culprit. Her sensual ability was certainly her weapon and she had him exactly where she wanted.

He still visited her in prison years later. He never asked her why she'd done it. In that point she was let off, but not in any of the others.

WE ALL HAVE QUALITIES!

Some people are good at pointing fingers.
Some people are good at telling white lies.
Some people are good at picking faults.
Some people are good at tripping up.
Some people are good at using daggers.
Some people are good at jumping in.
Some people are good at pulling hair.
Some people are good at throwing stones.
Some people are good at spitting.
Some people are good at stealing (and the limelight).
Some people are good at putting their nose in.
Some people are good at snatching.
Some people are good at impersonating snakes.
Some people are good at pushing in and/or out.
Some people are good at all of these.
Some people are good at none of these.
Some people are good at looking in the mirror every morning and smiling. . . .

HUNGRY

"How you welcome the sun when you've been starved of it!"
How you welcome anything you've been starved of – true love, actually.

TODAY'S SOCIETY

Lean and mean is IN.
Smoke and poke is OUT.
Shock and sock (it to them) is IN.
Spout and flout is OUT.
Tuck and suck is IN.
Mob* and sob is OUT.
Dance and prance is IN.

* Not everyone seems to know, so put the word out!

TOP GEAR

"Steroids didn't enhance my performance,
they just blew me up," he said.
It's a no-ball, otherwise they'll
blow away your chances . . .
of a complete blowout.

TIME OF DAY

You can usually tell someone
by their watch, they say.
Well, I must be
a right plain Jane,
who is still young at heart (fond of pink),
or
who just likes cheap and chic(?),
or
most certainly wants things from the home of the jewel and the crown.

10B

Just look at that bunch of kids in there! He's nitpicking. She's yawning. He's rolling up his sleeves. She's cleaning her glasses. He's gazing out of the window. She's twiddling her hair. He's scratching his foot. She's chatting about this 'n' that. He's wiping his brow. She's adjusting her skirt. He's poking in his ear. *She's listening to the teacher.* What do they have in common? They don't know what life has in store for them yet! She'll have it tough. He'll have it rough. She'll have a nice time. He'll have to sit and pine. She'll have to fight. He'll get a right fright. She'll break the hearts of many. He'll be lucky if he gets any.

WHO WOULD HAVE THOUGHT IT!

Who would have thought that this
little boy was to become so famous?
Who would have thought that this
little girl was to cure so many?
Who would have thought that this
little boy was to shine?
Who would have thought that this
little girl was to beat the system?

I did. We were pals once.

DID THE BAND TURN UP YET?

Seconds to halfway to midnight.
Sitting pretty.
Sitting straight (in the head).
Sitting tight around the legs.
Sitting by candle.
Sitting between speakers.
Sitting at (Arthur's) round table.
Sitting counting . . . but not cards, Kevin!

JUST IN TIME

Cry me a river.
Throw me a party.
Cook me a salad.
Pick me another car.
Hand me a can of beer.
Sling me my cap.
Look after my instruments.
Whatever you say, **Justin**!

ARE YOU THINKING WHAT I'M THINKING?

MY FIRST, MY LAST, MY EVERYTHING

"Spread them!"

And she did. And frequently. But this time it was different. The good-looking policeman pushed her against the car forcefully. She felt him. He felt her, but this time it was not to her liking. This time she was in deep shit.

And then it dawned on her. It was him. Her first, not her last, but her everything! He looked so different. And he acted that way. She was going to be his last, at least in his head. He was going to see to it that she would rot in hell, or wherever else she might like to rot.

She'd made problems for him. She'd ruined things for him. She'd caused him heartache beyond compare. It wasn't at all intentional. But that didn't make any difference to him. Revenge was written all over his face.

Neither of them moved an inch. She gasped. It was so intense. He just stared. She was starting to melt. The air was hot and thick and views were being impaired. They were alone in that garage. He'd planned it that way. She'd fallen for his pack of lies admirably.

And then his gun was at her head. She was going to quite literally lose her mind. She was now turning white. She was rigid. She was speechless. Her eyes were telling him to do whatever he wished. She saw no choice. He was cool, calm and collected.

He removed the gun and shot frantically around the room. He made sure he made his mark on every wall. He then grabbed her hair and pulled her towards him. His eyes were warm. His lips parted. They were very red. He kissed her. His fondle was too passionate for words. She responded. She was drenched.

And so they went shopping and nothing more was said. . . .

YOU CAN'T BE TOO CAREFUL THESE DAYS, LOVE

Well, who would have thought it! There she was talking to . . .
the man who sold the world,
a man who was locked up for an eternity,
a woman who is somewhere in between,
one of the richest men in the world,
the sweetest group around,
a woman who believes in the power of American natives,
a man who is going to Hollywood,
the man who bends it like no one else (at least on the pitch),
a woman who is looking for a big spender,
the man who is an illusion.

She didn't know them from Adam, but she does now:

David, (I),
Nelson,
Kate,
Bill ($$$$$$$$$$ and $$$$$$$$$$)
The 'all things nice' girls,
Linda,
Frankie,
David, (II),
Shirley,
Rob.

Keep clear of strangers cos you never know what might happen?!

CURTAINS

In the valley of death
I lay me to rest.
Given another chance
for what would I ask?
For a plate of love.
Love (hurts) heals.
And then I wouldn't pass away after all!

MOVING IN TIME

So thick the air with cigarettes.
It's filled with vibes of jazz too.
And the floor.
Can't see.
Can't move.
But they do and in time.
From side to side
with swinging hips.
Round and round
with flowing pleats of silk.
Back and forth
with points of shoes.
Red, purple, yellow, black and white
flashes before her eyes.
'Oh, how I adore you,' he thinks,
his hands stroking her curls.
Dreams of an endless night.
Chatting and laughing.
But they don't.
They just gaze into each other.

OUT OF THE BLUE

A job is rather like a moose really.
It pops up when you least expect it!
Well, all I can say is that mine is
a long time coming!
It must be lying shot and wounded somewhere.
Or is it still in the making . . . ?

SCREAM BLUE MURDER

I'll need to dress and go from here
if he is not coming back.
You may wish to talk;
I won't listen.
It will drive me insane.
So many deaf ears yesterday
(when my troubles seemed so far away to them).
Mine are today.
I'll be like Helen.
I'll no longer see the beauty
our planet offers.
I'll no longer hear the music.
I'll no longer find the words.

SECOND FIDDLE?

Love me for what I am,
not for what you want me to be.

For what you wanted me
to be . . . I am.

A major player.

WHEN 2 CALL IT A DAY

Freedom   **Revenge**

She cried for it.   He took it.
She took a chance.   He threw one.
She opened up.   He opened up.
She got back to herself. He turned for the worse.

They go hand in hand
just like walking down that aisle!

I DON'T NEED A SECOND OPINION

I don't need a second opinion
when I'm ordering my favourite dish
in my favourite restaurant,
when I'm choosing which colour
dress to wear,
when I'm deciding which dishy guy
to take home,
when I'm going to jump
twelve metres into water,
when I'm deciding to move cross-border.
But, I do when I'm going to have
the operation sure to change my life . . . !

ARE WE NEARLY DONE?

HAVE DREAMS, WILL FLY

"It wasn't enough!" she said.

"I wanted more!" she said.

He watched her walk away. He was transfixed. Who would have thought it. She didn't look the part. He was too embarrassed to say a word. Instead he turned and ran up the road to catch the bus he had almost missed.

The shrill voice of the skinhead sat in front of him seemed so far away. The trees were racing past, like his thoughts. His hands were clammy and he couldn't soothe the cruel throbbing, which was becoming more intense by the minute.

He had trouble concentrating on anything from that moment on. Such beautiful eyes. He never forgot those eyes. In fact he was hooked on just about every part of her anatomy. His nights were full of her in any amount of positions he could imagine.

Why did she walk off? Couldn't he have tried to keep her talking, if only so as to enjoy being under her spell for a while longer? Not much point when he had to be back by 7.30 p.m. It was fast approaching 7.25 p.m. already.

Surely his mother didn't still have that kind of a hold on him?! And at his age too! Well, it wasn't his mother. No, it was the guard! He was behind bars for framing the very woman causing the ache in his pants. She wanted more, but she wouldn't get it from him, not for a long, long time.

THE (CROSSWORD) SOLVERS' BOON

It's not just a dictionary.
It's a tribute to the indulgence of language lovers.
It's variety.
It's choices.
It's integration.
It's a balanced survey.
It's things banned.
It's things exalted.
It's a world to explore.

Are you talking about Mr Collins
lying on the table over there or about me?

THE FEAST

Sugar 'n' spice
and all things nice.
But who wants that when you can have mice?!
Big ones, small ones,
fat ones, thin ones
with deliciously lean tails.
I'll have a spider or two
if all else fails.
But bring me a cup of blood,
for it's better than a bowl of pud(ding).
I'll finish my meal
and sleepy I'll feel.
But no time to kip
cos it's . . . Halloween!

WHAT HAPPENED TO SUMMER?

It's been and gone.
What now?
We skipped over one.
We're already into the next.
So get ready for
frosty mornings,
dark days,
cosy evenings,
long nights.
And . . .
quickly jumping into clothes,
rushing through the flakes,
candles in every nook,
cuddling up for what seems like forever.

COLLECTIVELY

I am losing my faith.
But not in God.
Mankind.
I am losing it in that.
It's unkind.
And it's not my kind!
The rats are taking over the race.
Push, shove, trip, squeeze, cut,
tear, steal, trick, rip, squash.
Familiar moves.
Like opponents in chess.
I move it; you block it.
I win some; I lose some.
But, what's when you lose some
and . . . you lose some (more)?
It's no game.
A sad state of affairs!
So much more aware.
And I'm so numb.

HELLO, MR (EX) PRESIDENT

As the Americans would say:
Another day another dollar (bill).
Or in my case:
another day another bill,
but not a dollar and not Clinton either.

TOMORROW

My plans for the future?
To secure it for my children's sake.
My wishes for the future?
To be accepted.
To be included.
To finally be able / allowed
to spend time with those
where the chemistry between us
firmly bubbles. . . .

WHAT A BREAK (BIG BREAK)!

The only one I'm most likely to get
is either a tea break
or a Kit Kat!
Being broke means
there won't be a holiday either!
It could be away, down, even,
in, out, through or up.
Otherwise:
Being
Ready
Ensures
Applied
Karma!

(MEN) WOMAN AT WORK

She worked between Heaven and Earth.
The lake and the graveyard.
Heaven because that stretch of water
is just so beautiful.
And once you've had that view
from your window
you can't live without
that music to the ears, a lot maintain.
Earth because that's where
we go back to when we're done.
Done with
doing dirty dishes,
watching TV,
driving the kids (or theirs) to school,
talking to the neighbours,
making pancakes,
painting toenails,
writing postcards,
going to the WC.
Done with everything!

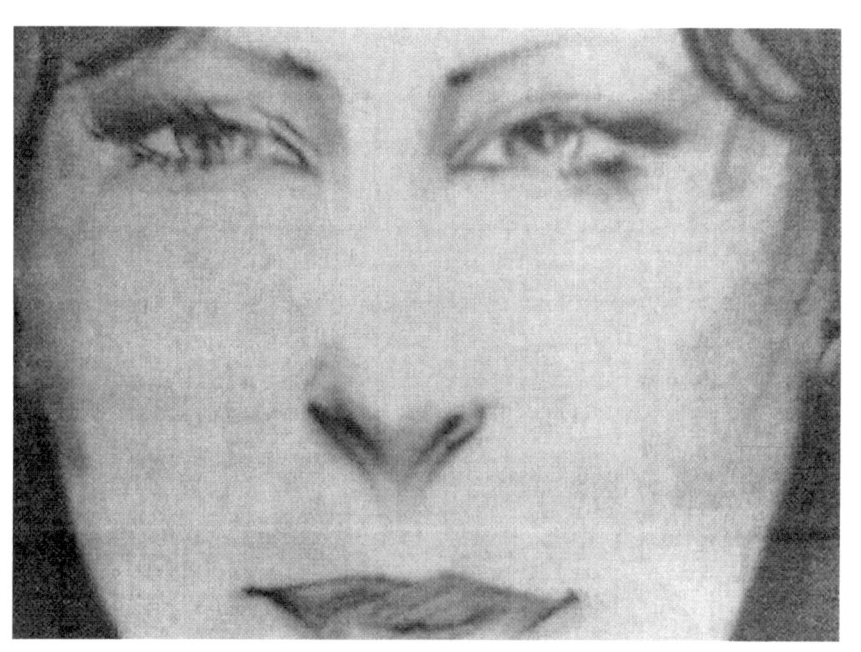

WHAT THE HECK!

SHORT BACK AND SIDES

If she'd wanted a haircut she would have gone to the hairdresser's. But he certainly made short work of it! There was no need or time for scissors. He just pulled it out, lump by lump. One could barely hear the row for the pounding of the beat downstairs. But she saw it. She was standing at the bottom of the stairs, clutching her Martini in white plastic. She was in awe until someone told her to move on and mind her own business. It was for the best, they said. But she was glued to her spot. She didn't know what to do. She felt for her. But, with a heavy heart, she soon returned to the others. By this time her interest in chilling had gone. It seemed like her suitor had deserted her, at least for a while. It was two very close to him who engaged her in some small talk. It was mostly about him and how untameable he usually was.

"You will be good for him," they said.

But after she came back from a prearranged month abroad on her own he was nowhere to be seen. Another drop in (over) the ocean!

YOU'LL END UP AS A BAR OF SOAP!

A woman with a number. Who was she anyway? She was a star. Well, at least she had one on her jacket. A fallen star, in fact. She often fell on the floor when being pushed around by those who thought they were superior and taking over. She didn't do much! Oh, but she did. She endured extreme pain. She let herself be degraded. She let herself be ridiculed. She let herself be made a spectacle of. She let herself be starved. She let herself be abused to save her next in line. But, they were next in the line! She changed the course of history. Who was she anyway? One of the six. Six? One of the six million remaining in that grave of a massive kind over there. I won't forget her and nor should you, your children or your children's children. Many often wonder what they will be in the next life. Such poor souls ended up in the bathrooms of thousands.

Cleansing takes on a whole new meaning, doesn't it?!

SHUT-EYE

I slept with Picasso all last week.
He caressed my weary locks.
He was all over my tired bones.
He kept me extremely warm
and I had very sweet dreams.
Don't worry – it's only my pillowcase and duvet cover!
(No disrespect meant, seeing as
how he shut his quite some time ago.)

FRUSTRATION GUARANTEED

Increase your sexual potential!
Excellent results immediately.
100% satisfaction or your money back.
Make life fun again!
Order now.

He lives alone.
And then what?!

LIVING IN A BOX

It does when it has that hard plastic over it.
So it doesn't get rammed hard
before it can get one on with Debra!

SWAN SONG

She was already late for her singing lesson. She had to put her foot on the gas. The motorway was busy. It was always a struggle to get out of work. It was always a rush to get there, but he wanted it that way. Upon arrival she parked up quickly and sprinted off down the track to the house. The light was on, but nobody was home. There was only the dog around the corner, which barked so ferociously that she didn't dare take a peep! She had lost her voice, but she didn't want to lose her face!

LET'S JAM IT

Sat there waiting for something . . .
noisy, fun, improvised, relaxed, vocal,
hot, dynamic, instrumental, local . . . to happen.

Godot didn't turn up, but they did!

LIFE – LOVE = A WASTE OF ONE

Life without love
Is like being in a closed box.
You can't see.
You can't touch.
You can't feel.
You can't give or take.
You lose all sense.

Break out and embrace it!
Cupid's gift.
Share it.
There is no better start . . . or finish.

MÉNAGE À TROIS

Three white matchstick angels hanging in the window.
If one white matchstick angel should accidentally fall
there'd be two white matchstick angels hanging in the window.

But that would be so sad.
We need all the angels we can get.
And not just at Christmas!
Not a man for all seasons, but an angel, Henry.

FOUR GREEN BOTTLES (A VARIATION)

There were four white toilet rolls standing on the ledge (in the WC).
There were four sexy ladies pouting their lips.
There were four fishermen with fishing rods picking their noses.
There were four cheeky schoolboys ripping heads off frogs.
There were four stuck-up grandmothers knitting woolly knickers.
There were four tired opera singers (the famous three plus one)
stuffing their faces with fish 'n' chips.
And if one should accidentally fall / collapse /
drown / choke / stab herself / die
... there'd be only three!

GIVE ME A SMILE, THEN!

* What's red in the face, foaming at the mouth and sweaty under the armpits?
Me, after having done a six-kilometre run in the middle of summer!

* What's wizened up and sitting between two humps?
Me, riding a camel across the desert on a 'dream of a lifetime' holiday which went slightly wrong!

* What's a darker shade of pale, climbing up the wall and doing an impersonation of a chainsaw?
Yours truly again! ('a day in the life of a mother' or 'just a day like any other'!)

Why the jokes?

Well, life is a bit of one really, isn't it?

THANKS FOR READING!